PRESENTED TO

_____

WITH LOVE FROM

_____

DATE

_____

Remember my words in your hearts and souls....
Talk about them when you sit at home
and walk along the road.
Talk about them when you lie down
and when you get up.

DEUTERONOMY 11:18–19

Illustrations copyright © Thomas Kinkade,
Media Arts Group, Inc., San Jose, CA

Text compilation copyright © 2001 by Tommy Nelson®,
a division of Thomas Nelson, Inc.

Published in Nashville, Tennessee, by Tommy Nelson®,
a division of Thomas Nelson, Inc.

Unless otherwise indicated, Scripture quotations are from the
International Children's Bible®, *New Century Version*®, copyright © 1986, 1988, 1999
by Tommy Nelson®, a division of Thomas Nelson, Inc. Used by permission.

ISBN 0-8499-7770-3

Library of Congress Control Number: 2001132130

Printed in China

01 02 03 04 05 LEO 5 4 3 2 1

THOMAS KINKADE

Favorite Bible Verses

Tommy NELSON

Thomas Nelson, Inc.
Nashville

"'Our Father in heaven,
we pray that your name will always be kept holy.

We pray that your kingdom will come.
We pray that what you want will be done,
here on earth as it is in heaven.

Give us the food we need for each day.

Forgive the sins we have done,
just as we have forgiven those
who did wrong to us.

Do not cause us to be tested;
but save us from the Evil One.'

Yes, if you forgive others
for the things they do wrong,
then your Father in heaven will also
forgive you for the things you do wrong.

But if you don't forgive the wrongs of others,
then your Father in heaven will not
forgive the wrongs you do."

MATTHEW 6:9–15

"For God loved the world so much that he gave his only Son. God gave his Son so that whoever believes in him may not be lost, but have eternal life."

JOHN 3:16

The Lord is my shepherd.
I have everything I need.

He gives me rest in green pastures.
He leads me to calm water.

He gives me new strength.
For the good of his name,
he leads me on paths that are right.

Even if I walk through a very dark valley,
I will not be afraid because you are with me.
Your rod and your walking stick comfort me.

You prepare a meal for me in front of my enemies.
You pour oil on my head.
You give me more than I can hold.

Surely your goodness
and love will be with me all my life.
And I will live in the house of the Lord forever.

PSALM 23:1–6

Give all your worries to him, because he cares for you.

I PETER 5:7

God's word is alive and working.
It is sharper than a sword sharpened on both sides.
It cuts all the way into us,
where the soul and the spirit are joined.
It cuts to the center of our joints and our bones.
And God's word judges the thoughts
and feelings in our hearts.

HEBREWS 4:12

Your word is like a lamp for my feet
and a light for my way.

PSALM 119:105

Do not be angry with each other, but forgive each other.
If someone does wrong to you, then forgive him.
Forgive each other because the Lord forgave you.

COLOSSIANS 3:13

Continue to ask, and God will give to you.
Continue to search, and you will find.
Continue to knock, and the door will open for you.

Yes, everyone who continues asking will receive.
He who continues searching will find.
And he who continues knocking
will have the door opened for him.

MATTHEW 7:7–8

Do for other people what you want them to do for you.

LUKE 6:31

I love you, Lord. You are my strength.

PSALM 18:1

Be kind and loving to each other.
Forgive each other just as God forgave you in Christ.

EPHESIANS 4:32

Forget about the wrong things people do to you.
You must not try to get even.
Love your neighbor as you love yourself.

LEVITICUS 19:18

As high as the sky is above the earth,
so great is his love for those who respect him.

PSALM 103:11

Give your worries to the Lord.
He will take care of you.
He will never let good people down.

PSALM 55:22

Give thanks to the God of heaven.
His love continues forever.

PSALM 136:26

We know that in everything God works for
the good of those who love him.

ROMANS 8:28

Yes, I am sure that nothing can
separate us from the love God has for us.
Not death, not life, not angels,
not ruling spirits, nothing now,
nothing in the future, no powers,
nothing above us, nothing below us,
or anything else in the whole world
will ever be able to separate us
from the love of God
that is in Christ Jesus our Lord.

ROMANS 8:38–39

Love the Lord your God with
all your heart, soul and strength.

DEUTERONOMY 6:5

But the Spirit gives love, joy,
peace, patience, kindness, goodness,
faithfulness, gentleness, self-control. . . .

Those who belong to Christ Jesus
have crucified their own sinful selves.
They have given up their old selfish feelings
and the evil things they wanted to do.

We get our new life from the Spirit.
So we should follow the Spirit.

GALATIANS 5:22–25

Look at the birds in the air.
They don't plant or harvest or store food in barns.
But your heavenly Father feeds the birds.
And you know that you are worth
much more than the birds.

MATTHEW 6:26

But the people who trust the Lord will become strong again.
They will be able to rise up as an eagle in the sky.
They will run without needing rest.
They will walk without becoming tired.

ISAIAH 40:31

Give thanks to the Lord because he is good.

His love continues forever.

PSALM 136:1

Each one should give, then,
what he has decided in his heart to give.
He should not give if it makes him sad.
And he should not give if he thinks he is forced to give.
God loves the person who gives happily.

2 CORINTHIANS 9:7

"I showed you in all things that you
should work as I did and help the weak.
I taught you to remember the words of Jesus.
He said, 'It is more blessed to give than to receive.'"

ACTS 20:35

"Don't judge other people, and you will not be judged.
Don't accuse others of being guilty,
and you will not be accused of being guilty.
Forgive other people, and you will be forgiven.
Give, and you will receive. . . ."

LUKE 6:37–38

Children, obey your parents
the way the Lord wants.
This is the right thing to do.

EPHESIANS 6:1

Do not worry about anything.
But pray and ask God for everything you need.
And when you pray, always give thanks.
PHILIPPIANS 4:6

Be full of joy in the Lord always. I will say again, be full of joy.
PHILIPPIANS 4:4

Always be happy.
Never stop praying.
Give thanks whatever happens.
That is what God wants for you in
Christ Jesus.

1 THESSALONIANS 5:16–18

Love is patient and kind.
Love is not jealous,
it does not brag,
and it is not proud.

Love is not rude, is not selfish,
and does not become angry easily.
Love does not remember
wrongs done against it.

Love is not happy with evil,
but is happy with the truth.

Love patiently accepts all things.
It always trusts, always hopes,
and always continues strong.

1 CORINTHIANS 13:4–7

So go and make followers of all people in the world.
Baptize them in the name of the Father
and the Son and the Holy Spirit.

MATTHEW 28:19

Forget about the wrong things people do to you.
You must not try to get even.
Love your neighbor as you love yourself.

LEVITICUS 19:18

Index of Paintings